# Camping Fun

by C.L. Reid
illustrated by Elena Aiello

PICTURE WINDOW BOOKS
a capstone imprint

Published by Picture Window Books, a Capstone imprint
1710 Roe Crest Drive
North Mankato, Minnesota 56003
capstonepub.com

Copyright © 2025 by Capstone
All rights reserved. No part of this publication may be reproduced in whole or in part, or stored in a retrieval system, or transmitted in any form or by any means, electronic, mechanical, photocopying, recording, or otherwise, without written permission of the publisher.

Library of Congress Cataloging-in-Publication Data
Names: Reid, C. L., author. | Aiello, Elena (Illustrator), illustrator.
Title: Camping fun / by C.L. Reid ; illustrated by Elena Aiello.
Description: North Mankato, Minnesota : Picture Window Books, 2025. | Series: Emma every day | Audience: Ages 5-7. | Audience: Grades K-1. | Summary: Emma, who is deaf and uses sign language to communicate, enjoys a summer camping trip with her family. Includes an ASL fingerspelling chart and sign language guide.
Identifiers: LCCN 2023039280 (print) | LCCN 2023039281 (ebook) | ISBN 9781484692882 (hardcover) | ISBN 9781484692899 (paperback) | ISBN 9781484692943 (kindle edition) | ISBN 9781484692950 (epub) | ISBN 9781484693056 (pdf) Subjects: CYAC: Deaf—Fiction. | People with disabilities—Fiction. | Camps—Fiction. | Camping—Fiction. | Family life—Fiction. | LCGFT: Picture books. Classification: LCC PZ7.1.R4544 Cam 2024 (print) | LCC PZ7.1.R4544 (ebook) | DDC [E]—dc23
LC record available at https://lccn.loc.gov/2023039280
LC ebook record available at https://lccn.loc.gov/2023039281

Image Credits: Capstone: Randy Chewning, 28 (top, both), 29 (top right, bottom left), Daniel Griffo, 28 (bottom left), Mick Reid, 28 (bottom right), 29 (top left, bottom right)

Design Elements: Shutterstock: achii, Mari C, Mika Besfamilnaya

Special thanks to Evelyn Keolian for her consulting work.

Editor's note: Throughout the book, a few words are called out and fingerspelled using ASL. Some of these words do have signs as well.

Designer: Bobbie Nuytten

# TABLE OF CONTENTS

Chapter 1
## Setting Up Camp............................ 8

Chapter 2
## The Hike...........................................14

Chapter 3
## The Beach..................................... 20

# MEET EMMA

## EMMA CARTER
Age: 8   Grade: 3

### SIBLING

One brother, Jaden
(12 years old)

### PARENTS
David and Lucy

### BEST FRIEND
Izzie Jackson

### PET
a goldfish named Ruby

favorite color: teal
favorite food: tacos
favorite school subject: writing
favorite sport: swimming
hobbies: reading, writing, biking, swimming

# FINGERSPELLING GUIDE

## MANUAL ALPHABET

Aa     Bb     Cc     Dd     Ee

Ff     Gg     Hh     Ii     Jj

## MANUAL NUMBERS

0     1     2     3

Emma is Deaf. She uses American Sign Language (ASL) to communicate with her family. She also uses a Cochlear Implant (CI) to help her hear.

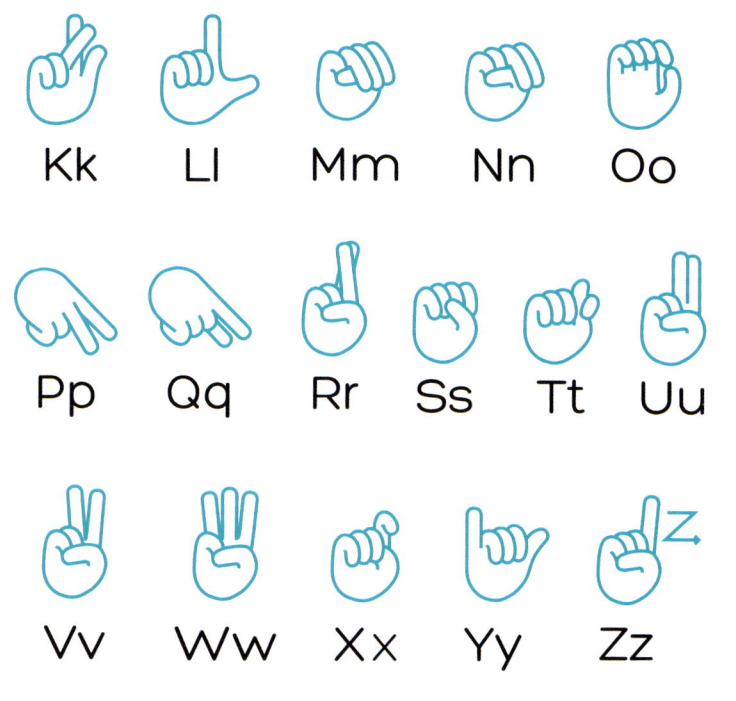

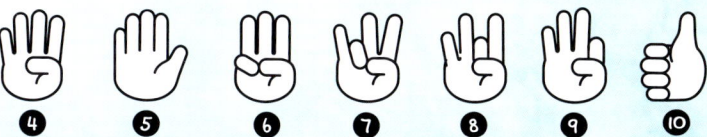

Chapter 1

# Setting Up Camp

Emma and her family had been in the car all day. At last, they turned onto a gravel road.

Thick trees grew on both sides of the road. Emma saw a lake. She saw a sign too.

"We are here!" Emma signed.

Mom and Dad checked in at the main office. They got their campsite number. They got a list of activities to try too.

Dad drove past lots of campsites. They finally found their site. It had a picnic table and a firepit.

"It is getting late. We should set things up," Mom signed.

"I will help with the tent," Emma signed.

Emma and her mom found a good spot. The ground was level. The grass was thick and soft.

"I will collect sticks for the fire," Jaden signed.

"I will set up the hammocks," Dad signed.

Everyone worked fast. Camp was set up in no time!

Emma looked over the activity list. There were so many fun things to do!

"Can we look for shooting stars tonight?" Emma signed.

"Good idea," Mom signed.

## Chapter 2
# The Hike

The next morning, the family went for a hike. They saw berries and flowers. They saw bugs. They even saw a waterfall!

"It is time to head back for lunch," Mom signed.

"Follow me," Emma signed.

Emma skipped ahead. When she rounded a bend in the path, she stopped.

A doe and a fawn stood on the path. Emma could not believe it!

Jaden, Mom, and Dad caught up with Emma. They quietly watched the deer.

A small noise scared the deer, and they took off.

"This is the best day ever!" Emma signed.

"I agree," Jaden signed.

"And it is just going to get better," Dad signed.

For lunch, Dad cooked hot dogs over the fire. Jaden set the table. Mom put out grapes and carrots. Emma added some chips.

"I like camp food," Emma signed.

"Me too," Jaden signed.

After lunch and some rest time, the family got ready for the beach. They packed sunblock, towels, sand toys, and snacks. Emma packed the activity list too.

"Let's go!" Dad signed.

Chapter 3
# The Beach

After a short walk, Emma saw the lake. She saw a sandy beach and a dock.

"It is perfect," Emma signed.

"Yes it is," Mom signed.

Emma took off her Cochlear Implant (CI). She didn't want to get it wet.

"Let's go swimming," Emma signed.

She ran to the water. Jaden followed. Mom and Dad watched.

After swimming and a snack, Emma put her CI back on. Then she looked at the list again.

"Let's search for treasure," Emma signed.

"After that, we should build a sandcastle," Jaden signed.

They walked along the beach. Emma found lots of cool rocks. Jaden found cool shells.

"Let's use these treasures on our sandcastle," Jaden signed.

"Good idea," Emma signed.

Emma and Jaden built a big sandcastle. They used the rocks and shells to make it fancy.

"Wow!" Dad signed.

"That is impressive," Mom signed.

The sun began to set. They packed up and started back to camp. Everyone was tired and hungry.

After dinner, they had a bonfire. B-O-N-F-I-R-E They toasted marshmallows.

"Tasty!" Jaden signed.

"And messy," Emma signed.

Emma looked at the list again.

She checked off lots of activities.

"Look at everything we did," Emma signed.

"And we will do even more tomorrow," Dad signed.

"I can't wait!" Emma signed.

# LEARN TO SIGN

### bug

Put thumb on nose and bend fingers.

### family

Make F shapes and move hands in a circle.

### happy

Make two small circles at chest.

### sand

Rub fingers together.

## swimming

Move hands in small circles.

## towel

Move fists back and forth.

## tree

Wiggle wrist back and forth.

## water

Make W shape and tap mouth twice.

# GLOSSARY

**Cochlear Implant (CI)**—a device that helps someone who is deaf to hear; it is worn on the head just above the ear

**deaf**—being unable to hear

**doe**—a female deer

**fawn**—a young deer

**fingerspell**—to make letters with your hands to spell out words; often used for names of people and places

**level**—a flat, even spot

**sign language**—a language in which hand gestures, along with facial expressions and body movements, are used to communicate

**site**—spot or location

## TALK ABOUT IT

1. Would you want to go camping? Why or why not?

2. Emma camps with her family. Talk about something fun you do with your family.

3. Camping is a good way to get outside and enjoy nature. Why is it important to spend time outside?

## WRITE ABOUT IT

1. Make a list of at least five things you like to do outside.

2. You can camp in any season. Pick a season. Write a paragraph about why it would be fun to camp during that time of year.

3. There are lots of different types of camps, from sports to theater. Write about a camp you would like to attend.

## ABOUT THE AUTHOR

Deaf-blind since childhood, C.L. Reid received a Cochlear Implant (CI) as an adult to help her hear, and she uses American Sign Language (ASL) to communicate. She and her husband have three sons. Their middle son is also deaf-blind. Reid earned a master's degree in writing for children and young adults at Hamline University in St. Paul, Minnesota. Reid lives in Minnesota with her husband, two of their sons, and their cats.

## ABOUT THE ILLUSTRATOR

Elena Aiello is an illustrator and character designer. After graduating as a marketing specialist, she decided to study art direction and CGI. Doing so, she discovered a passion for illustration and conceptual art. She works as a freelancer for various magazines and publishers. Aiello loves video games and sushi and lives with her husband and her little pug, Gordon, in Milan, Italy.